Mini Sagas

Mini Marvels

TALES FROM LANCASHIRE

First published in Great Britain in 2010 by
Young Writers, Remus House, Coltsfoot Drive,
Peterborough, PE2 9JX
Tel (01733) 890066 Fax (01733) 313524
Website: www.youngwriters.co.uk

Disclaimer
Young Writers has maintained every effort
to publish stories that will not cause offence.
Any stories, events or activities relating to individuals
should be read as fictional pieces and not construed
as real-life character portrayal.

Foreword

Since Young Writers was established in 1990, our aim has been to promote and encourage written creativity amongst children and young adults. By giving aspiring young authors the chance to be published, Young Writers effectively nurtures the creative talents of the next generation, allowing their confidence and writing ability to grow.

With our latest fun competition, *The Adventure Starts Here ...* , secondary school children nationwide were given the tricky challenge of writing a story with a beginning, middle and an end in just fifty words.

The diverse and imaginative range of entries made the selection process a difficult but enjoyable task with stories chosen on the basis of style, expression, flair and technical skill. A fascinating glimpse into the imaginations of the future, we hope you will agree that this entertaining collection is one that will amuse and inspire the whole family.

Contents

West Craven High Technology College, Barnoldswick

The Mini Sagas

The Bogeyman

He's hiding in your shed, or even under your bed! You know he can't be trusted and never be busted! He watches you in the day and taunts you at night. If you say the wrong thing he will give you a fright! You know he can dance!

Mark Bell-Porter (11)
Montgomery High School, Blackpool

Race Against Time

Running for her life, Rachel felt like her lungs were about to burst. She could feel the enemy advancing on her. She couldn't let them get to her. She ran faster still, trying to shake them off. Finally she got there.

'Once again Rachel Evans speeds into first place. Excellent!'

Maya Dewhurst (12)

Montgomery High School, Blackpool

2

Late

Amy's bus was late. She knew by the time she got there she would be five minutes late. Too much for Mr Sease. She saw some 50p chocolate and ran to school.
Standing outside the door she had her excuse ready; took a deep breath and opened the handle …
'*Late!*'

Bethany Butters (11)
Montgomery High School, Blackpool

3

Untitled

Once there was a lonely, hairy beetle. He had no friends as he was the town drunk. All he did was drink, drink and drink. His name was Thomas the Drunk. One day he was strolling along and he fell over and banged his head very hard. He was hurt.

Matthew Drinkwater (12)
Montgomery High School, Blackpool

The Grass Is Blue, The Sky Is Green

I woke up. The sky was green, the grass was blue. It looked very odd. I went to the doctor and he said it had always been like that. I was very confused. I had lunch, then looked out the window. The sky was blue, the grass was green.

Aaron Trickovic (12)
Montgomery High School, Blackpool

5

Untitled

Tom ran as fast as he could to get away from the crazed dog. He ran into the abandoned house. The dog followed. He climbed out of the balcony and something fell out of his pocket. *Beef jerky*. The dog left Tom for the beef jerky Tom was relieved.

Daniel Hart (11)
Montgomery High School, Blackpool

Joe And Dexy And The Minotaur

One day a little king visited Joe and Dexy and
demanded that they kill the Minotaur. If not they
must die themselves!
So Dexy and Joe set off on a great adventure to
kill the Minotaur. They sailed through the strong
seas, then killed the Minotaur.

Joseph Evans & Dexy Thornley (11)
Montgomery High School, Blackpool

7

The Minotaur

The Minotaur steamed at Josh. Josh quickly jumped up a tree to hide. Lots of trees grew in the forest. Suddenly the Minotaur ran, making the tree fall to the ground. Josh now had to face him or run. Josh stood tall and the Minotaur stopped running; staring at Josh …

Adam Hope (11)
Montgomery High School, Blackpool

The Monkeys

One day there was a monkey called Fruity. He loved bananas. His friend stopped by and ate all his bananas. Fruity was not happy and went to his friend's house and told him they couldn't be friends anymore. His friend put the bananas back and they were both friends again.

Jemma Green (12)
Montgomery High School, Blackpool

Jelly Legs

He stumbled, desperately trying to walk. His legs were not reacting. It was like he had strings attached and a puppeteer was pulling them. A warm, gentle nuzzle touched his small, delicate body. The fawn calmed down and with a lot of hard work, walked slowly towards his mother deer.

Molly Wilkinson (12)
Montgomery High School, Blackpool

Untitled

One day I woke up and had butterflies in my stomach. I felt energetic and I needed to play with a football. My phone buzzed and I was told I was playing footy at Anfield.
Once I got there it was nearly time for kick-off. We won!

Michael Spence & Lewis Maney-Roskell (12)
Montgomery High School, Blackpool

11

Untitled

One day I woke up and I was David Beckham. I was really shocked to be in such a big house and I saw Victoria Beckham next to me. I said, 'Hello, how are you?'

She replied, 'I'm good. Isn't it time for you to go to your amazing football?'

Andrew Grogan (11)
Montgomery High School, Blackpool

Puppy Job

Suddenly I was pounced on, a slobbering lick all up my face, and then another one. I didn't know how the cage of puppies had been released off the latch. I really should have put the dog food down. I know I am quitting this job!

Danielle Wright (12)
Montgomery High School, Blackpool

13

The Attic

There was a sound, a sound I couldn't explain. It sounded like someone whispering, *'Be warned!'* I felt a chill creeping down my back. I thought to myself, *what is lurking in this attic?* I was quietly tiptoeing around this cluttered, jumbled-up attic, suddenly the door *locked!*

Chloe Astin-Tripyear (11)
Montgomery High School, Blackpool

14

The Friendly Holiday

One sunny day, me and my friends went abroad to the Maldives. We decided to go and have a look in a cave which lead to a forest. We had a walk through the forest, then me and Megan heard a loud scream. Abi and Gaby had fallen down a hole!

Kathryn Lomas (12)

Montgomery High School, Blackpool

15

The Ghost House

Taylor was running down the corridor with his eyes closed, his heart was thumping against his ribs. He knew he had to get out of this house. He opened his eyes. The tattered old furniture was ripped and toppled over. He looked over his shoulder - there was a loud scream ...

Joseph West (12)

Montgomery High School, Blackpool

Sam The Hero

One day Sam woke up and heard someone
screaming outside. He looked out of his window
and saw a girl who had fallen over. Sam quickly
ran outside to help her. He took her inside,
cleaned her up and put a plaster on her. Sam is
the hero next door.

Sam Fletcher (11)
Montgomery High School, Blackpool

The Red Mustang

The boy woke up on a warm, sunny day in Florida. There were posh cars driving up and down, the sun sparkling off their new paint. The crackling of the exhaust echoing off the mountains. The low body kits were low enough to kiss the road.

Samuel Brown (11)
Montgomery High School, Blackpool

Hook's Mistake

Peter Pan woke up in a pool of blood. He noticed that the blood was coming from Captain Hook's room. He went in and found Tinkerbell staring at Hook. 'What happened?' asked Peter.
'He picked his nose with the wrong hand!' replied Tinkerbell.
'Bad way to go!' said Peter.

Taylor Gradwell (12)
Montgomery High School, Blackpool

The Wood Dragon

There is a little tale about a ferocious wood dragon. Is it a myth? No one knows.
The wood dragon is big and small, dark green camouflaged. It lives in the forest looking for prey and can't breathe fire, or he would be found. Unfortunately he hasn't been.

Josh Stanton (12)

Montgomery High School, Blackpool

Alex Hicks And The Headless Minotaur

One night Alex had a dream. He dreamt of fighting the Minotaur. He was in a cave, a dark cave. There were noises all around him. He saw a light at the end. He ran towards it. He could make out a figure. The headless Minotaur! He froze ...

Josuah Blakemore (11)
Montgomery High School, Blackpool

21

Banana Game

Far, far away lived a banana. It jumped over a wall and landed on its head. It went to hospital. The doctor said, 'Rest, you need an operation.'
The banana went home and got in the bath and lived happily ever after.

Jake Baldwin (11)
Montgomery High School, Blackpool

22

Ghost

It was Christmas Eve. Mum, Katie and me were in the front room listening to music. We were eating food and could hear the telly through the radio and I said, 'If anyone else is here, turn up the volume?' The volume went up full blast. I cried!

Ebony Samm (11)
Montgomery High School, Blackpool

23

The Chase

The heroic boy pursued the bloodthirsty vampire into the total blackness. Cobwebs hung across archways. He was blind, like a bat. Lightning flashed as the chase gained pace. Ghouls and ghosts flew past him. He was consumed with fear. The creaky door opened … the ride ended. £2 well spent!

Bradley Irving (12)
Montgomery High School, Blackpool

Gone!

Jake was playing outside when he saw the woman with her dogs again. So he went to play with the dogs. She said, 'Come and see my cats, they're lovely.' So Jake went into the woman's house, not knowing the dangers of what would happen. Jake was never seen again!

James Kellett (11)
Montgomery High School, Blackpool

The Washing Machine

Steve's washing machine was amazing; turn it on and step inside. You could travel back and forth in time like the TARDIS in Doctor Who. Steve programmed the washing machine to travel to the future where cars fly. *'Wow!'* Steve gasped. He got back in time for tea at 6pm.

Natalie Kay (12)

Montgomery High School, Blackpool

Where Did The Starfish Go?

Many years ago I created my own starfish. When
he outgrew his fish bowl, (then the sink), I kindly
grabbed him by one arm and placed him firmly in
the nearby rock pool, down the road.
Next I heard on the news my starfish was
disturbing crabs in the ocean!

Rebecca Leyland (12)
Montgomery High School, Blackpool

Creature Of The Dark

In the darkest spot of the forest, a dark creature
jumped out from the bush and jumped on top of
a rock, on a mountain.
His back was straight and his lips red with blood;
the moonlight shining on him. The creature gave
up again. (That's all folks!)

Jack Shaw (11)
Montgomery High School, Blackpool

The Return Of Pacman

In a random place called Funland, there lived a guy called Jim Bob Jr. He got savagely attacked by Pacman, who then went to the shop and gobbled up the shopkeeper called Jim Bob Jr 4. He was then savagely killed all over the stock. How grim!

Mark Watt (12)

Montgomery High School, Blackpool

The Way King Julius Died

This story begins in Rome. King Julius, the ruler of the country, was walking near the river that surrounded his palace. A servant pushed Julius into his famous river that no one was allowed to trek by. King Julius had no way of getting out of the river. He drowned.

Shannon Williamson (12)
Montgomery High School, Blackpool

Cracked

Humpty-Dumpty was bored on a cool day. Then he saw the biggest wall ever. He wanted to climb on it so badly, so he climbed the wall. He felt like the king of the world but one clumsy fall caused him to come crashing down to the floor, then *crack!*

James Abbass (12)
Montgomery High School, Blackpool

The World's Best Hero

Afro Man, the world's best hero. There was a girl around, she was only two years old. A man called Scissors came and kidnapped her. Afro Man ran after him. He quickly caught the girl but not Scissors, so there is still a job to be done for Afro Man.

Jonathan Brown (12)
Montgomery High School, Blackpool

Jack And His Axe

Jack went up the hill to fetch a pail of water. He went back to sell his crown for some magic beans. Jack awoke the giant when he grew the stalk. The giant climbed down to eat him with his fork, but Jack hacked down the stalk. Hooray! Hooray!

Callum Daniels (12)

Montgomery High School, Blackpool

33

Woof, Woof, Pink Dog

'Woof, woof, pink dog, have you any fur?'
'Yes ma'am, yes ma'am, five boxes full. Three for
the three children who live up the hill. One for
the bear who lives over there. So ma'am there
is one box left, would you care to take it off my
hands? *Woof!*'

Ellie Hornsby (11)
Montgomery High School, Blackpool

If The Wind Changes

Mia stared at the old man in horror. He was wearing an old, grey suit and glasses. He spoke quite posh and was concerned about Mia's face. 'If the wind changes you'll stay like that forever,' said the man. Mia then realised that the man was her dead great grandfather ...

Sophie Booth (12)

Montgomery High School, Blackpool

35

The Chase

The mouse was scampering in front of his enemy.
The cat! So round the garden they ran. Then
the cat stopped at his enemy's paws with claws
on the end … The dog! So all the animals were
chasing round the garden. Will it be over?
'Paws, Boots! Come here again!'

Abigail Hill (11)
Montgomery High School, Blackpool

Sally And Jim!

Sally and Jim sat on a wall. Jim was unfortunate
and had a great fall and Sally didn't know, and
carried on what she was doing. Jim shouted,
'Help, Sally!'
She ran to get all the elephants and all the queens.
All the elephants and queens put Jim together
again.

Jordan Davies (12)
Montgomery High School, Blackpool

37

Morning Swim

One day Jack was swimming in the clear blue
sea. The beach was dead. *Empty*, he thought to
himself, *why is no one here?*
The sea was still. Unaware the sea was inhabited
with jellyfish. 'Argh!' He had been stung. He
drowned slowly and painfully. Nobody knew he
was there.

Shola Welch (11)

Montgomery High School, Blackpool

Cloud Nine

Tilly was swept off her feet. She awoke to find
herself in a world of clouds … their heads on
springs, bouncing. She heard a loud, thunderous
crash. She approached a large, dark house.
Creeping through the door, there suddenly came
a rather loud scream … The door slammed
behind her …

Nicole Moore (12)

Montgomery High School, Blackpool

39

Oblivion

Jimmy stared down into the deep, dark hole below. Oblivion - one big vertical drop, the tallest roller coaster in Britain. 'It only lasts ten seconds,' he whispered to himself nervously. 'Here we go!' he screamed.

'Wake up Jimmy,' whispered his mum. Jimmy woke up outside Alton Towers - the home of Oblivion.

Luke Stevenson (12)
Montgomery High School, Blackpool

The Terrifying Reflection

Skye jumped up on the worktop, she thought she saw dinner; Chloe, the fish. Skye's paw met the water, Chloe was whirling nervously round the bowl, thinking she would never see tomorrow. Suddenly Skye spotted something in the corner of her eye, Lisa, her owner, came in. 'Down Skye!'

Emily Bradbury (11)
Montgomery High School, Blackpool

41

Fusion!

As they stepped into the queue of the new roller coaster, Fusion. Their hearts pounded with fear and excitement. The blazing sun of a Florida morning, shone brightly on them. Katie and Emma slowly crawled into the seats of Fusion. It started. As they crawled to the top … *bang!*

Hannah Newell (11)

Montgomery High School, Blackpool

The Voice

As the door slowly opened, John peered his head
round the crooked door. The light turned on
and started to flicker rapidly! John jumped back,
shaking with fear. He started running to the door.
'Stop!' shouted a voice! 'I need to speak to you!'
'What do you want with me?'

Ailish Eaves (12)
Montgomery High School, Blackpool

43

The Ghost House

The door creaked slowly as he entered the house. Joe suddenly felt very small in this darkened place. There were knives, ghosts and ghouls everywhere. He had never been so scared. Unexpectedly a dark shadow emerged from the depths. 'Hello,' he shouted. 'Where's the gift shop?'

Never again, Joe thought.

Christopher Tayib (11)
Montgomery High School, Blackpool

Melvin's Journey

Melvin, the monkey, had travelled through places whilst also encountering many faces. From every continent to the capital of France, each step he took contained a prance. After searching high and low, he saw a little yellow glow. A banana with a tangy smell which he did deserve as well!

Ecem Ozturk (11)

Montgomery High School, Blackpool

45

Alone In The Dark

'Twas a dark night, the moon was out. The man walked cautiously down the street. He stopped. There was a rustling noise … he carried on … the gate opened and slammed shut. Nothing. He continued. Suddenly he felt breathing on his neck. Would he see another day?

Henry Walsh (12)
Montgomery High School, Blackpool

The Shadows

Gone in a second, no trace, no explanation. The intermingled thorns twisted around the frail path. I crept carefully, the old oak tree swishing and waving to me, memories flooded back, the newly cut grass. I stopped. A whirlwind of silhouettes danced up the crusty wall. Was I seeing things?

Elizabeth Burns (11)
Montgomery High School, Blackpool

A Day In The Life Of Pasty Patricia And Melon Maunder

Melon Maunder and Pasty Patricia walk into the banquet room and walk up to the food and start to sing, 'Food, glorious food! I love food!' 'Cut!' yells Director Dale. 'It needs more umph! Everyone take five and Julie, call my therapist *now!* Oh and get me a frothachino, darling.'

Sharna Harrison (11)

Montgomery High School, Blackpool

Falling Nightmare

They pulled over next to the cliff and quietly stepped out. The three children and their mother crept round to the back of the car. 'Mother, why are we pushing the car off the cliff?' asked one of the children quietly.

'Sshhh, you'll wake your father up!' replied the mother …

Jack Moulson (12)

Montgomery High School, Blackpool

49

The Big Drop

Isobel swung and tried to jump onto a branch. She missed again! She knew she was going to fall, so she kept trying. Suddenly, the branch started to lean at a strange angle. Then it snapped and fell to the hard, rocky ground! And so did Isobel.

Lucy Dacosta (12)
Montgomery High School, Blackpool

Keep Running

The man kept running. 'I thought it was just a myth,' said the man, running faster, away from the beastly creature. He was running towards the main part of Hack Town. The man ran into a shop. He heard a noise, looked up to see the creature staring at him ...

Thomas Gore (12)

Montgomery High School, Blackpool

The Machine

Bella stared in horror at the machine. People were screaming as it twisted and turned, getting higher and higher. Bella's heart was pounding. She was next … She saw her friend on it screaming with her hands in the air. The machine stopped. She couldn't wait to go on the Whirlwind!

Amy Donovan (12)
Montgomery High School, Blackpool

Untitled

'Twas the night before Halloween and all was
quiet, as the beast lurked beneath the sewers.
The streetlamps flickered and the beast returned.
The people of Miniko quivered as their stomachs
churned. Cloaked like the clouds, it lurked
through the streets. It wanted to eat. Grey-faced
and ... gone!

Benjamin Kinnon (12)
Montgomery High School, Blackpool

Mouse Trap!

Step by step, creak by creak, terrified, grey
mouse scurried away with its heart in its mouth.
The jaws of the gigantic monster chased after it.
Its metal teeth clanked against its wooden body.
The mouse swerved quickly into its hole …
turned out it was only a trap!

Charmaine Attwater (11)

Montgomery High School, Blackpool

Ghost Foal

Sancho ran along the sandy shore. He felt a
breeze but 'twas very poor. The sun shone out
loud and bright. He turned around as he had a
fright. There was his mother standing tall. He
steadied himself as he began to fall.
'Twas all a dream after eating cream …

Kelsey Smith (11)
Montgomery High School, Blackpool

The Bloody Hoof

The horse tripped over a rock. She stumbled onto the concrete ground. Her hoof bled, red silky blood. The horse got up and carried on, limping to the golden beach. At the beach, she flopped onto the ground, her hoof bleeding even more. Lying there she neighed, no one came …

Lizzy Baseley (12)
Montgomery High School, Blackpool

Whoops!

Me and my friends Kathryn, Abi and Gaby all went for a walk along the promenade. We stopped off at the ice cream shop. We sat down, started talking and forgot about time. 'I need to go!' Gaby ran away. 'Argh!' Aby had run into a lamp post while running!

Megan Hambly (12)
Montgomery High School, Blackpool

57

The Beast

The beady, red eyes glared at me as I slowly backed away towards the door. I frantically turned the door handle. Locked! Suddenly a flash of bright light beamed through the window. There was a clash, then a cloud of dust rushed past me. Had the beastly creature disappeared forever?

Rebecca Gray (12)
Montgomery High School, Blackpool

Run For Your Life

The giant, frightening monster glared at the small,
weak child. His teeth were as sharp as knives,
sticking out of his dribbling mouth. The child ran
as fast as his little legs could carry him but every
twenty steps he did, the monster did one! The
monster grabbed him …

James Bartholomew (11)
Montgomery High School, Blackpool

The Abandoned House

As Martin was walking home, he saw a deserted house he had never seen before. He really didn't want to go in and he knew he shouldn't have but he was just so curious. He walked in and heard a tapping sound. He was scared to go any further in …

Ben Lewis (11)
Montgomery High School, Blackpool

The Dragon's Den

The dragon slept in total darkness, surrounded
by bones of the forgotten. Smoke was coming
from all entrances and exits of the castle. There
was a sudden clatter of metal, it was yet another
knight. He snuck up to the dragon and … *slice,*
the dreaded creature was no more.

Luke Powell (11)
Montgomery High School, Blackpool

The Interrogation

Jacob sat in the chair opposite his prisoner and stared into her deep blue eyes. 'What are you hiding?' he whispered threateningly. He could see she was about to break, her throat clenched, a bead of sweat ran softly down her forehead. Suddenly she yelled, 'Alright, I ate your cookie!'

George Kerwood (12)

Montgomery High School, Blackpool

Forever

Forever goes on and on and on and on, from the old Romans, to new technology, developing methods to how and why, because nothing happens until you try. It's nothing money can buy. You have a life, then it's gone! But forever goes on and on and on and on and on!

Gabrielle Richards (11)
Montgomery High School, Blackpool

The Enchanted Forest

I wandered through the enchanted forest. I finally saw what was so magical; the fountain! It was beautiful. Suddenly the sky went black. The sun disappeared and the life beneath me began to die. I didn't know what to do. I saw something behind me. The door slammed shut.

Hannah Norton (11)

Montgomery High School, Blackpool

The Shadow

It was a dark, foggy evening. There was a shadow in the distance. It approached Lydia slowly. Lydia backed away from the shadow. It continued to pace itself towards Lydia. Lydia was about to run home when she recognised the shadow.
'Oh Claire! I didn't see you there!' Lydia said.

Emily Buzza (11)
Montgomery High School, Blackpool

Soldier Boy

As he crept forward, gun at the ready, he heard glass crack beneath his feet. As he opened the door, he heard *crash*, as a bullet hit his head. He fell down dying, blood everywhere.
'James, tea is ready!' He sat forward, turned it off and ran downstairs.

Flinn Tetlow (11)
Montgomery High School, Blackpool

The Bogeyman!

He'll whisper your name ... 'Billy ... Billy ... pull
down your covers,' and then ... *he'll get you!*
'Have a nice sleep,' whispered Ben, as he left the
room. Ben went to bed and fell asleep.
'Ben ... ' Ben's covers fell to the floor.
'Rahhh!'
'Argh!'
'Ha-ha, have a nice sleep!' said Billy.

Hayley Walsh (12)
Montgomery High School, Blackpool

The Shipwreck

The big queen ship crashed onto the island. Jack saw some people. He walked over, they were cutting and be-heading animals! Jack started to run nearer and one of them looked at him with meat in his hands and blood on his face. He said, 'Don't you want some?'

Jake Ashton (12)

Montgomery High School, Blackpool

Parkour

Running over the rooftops, adrenaline rushing
through his body, wind rushing against his face,
giving him a headache. He persevered, continuing
over the skyscrapers of New York City. Dark
clouds formed overhead like evil candyfloss. The
rain came down. A rushing sensation, then there
was just darkness.

Caleb Curtis (12)

Montgomery High School, Blackpool

Snakes On A Plane

It was a nice, comfy journey on a plane when suddenly there was a loud hissing sound coming from under the seats. Everyone started screaming as they could see a man on the floor covered in at least one hundred snakes eating his flesh. *Hssss!* Fifty-two humans left.

Luke Pinder (11)

Montgomery High School, Blackpool

The Day She Disappeared

One dull, miserable day Beth was walking down
the road when something grabbed her leg. What
could it be? Maybe a monster? 'Argh!' shouted
Beth as the monster-like thing grabbed her by
the foot. What could have happened to her?
Something bad probably, as she was never seen
again!

Holly Pearson (11)
Montgomery High School, Blackpool

71

Baked

Peter stood back as he watched the unknown
figure in the white coat punch and jab and slice
the object on the counter. Blood splattered
everywhere. The figure turned around. Hiding
behind the counter, I watched him put the
mysterious object in the oven.
Thirty minutes later: 'Jam doughnut sir?'

Liam Herrador (12)
Montgomery High School, Blackpool

The World's End

The dream was always the same. It started happy and ended sad. She couldn't see much but the sounds were horrific. The sound of a bullet leaving a gun, then silence. Not a normal silence, an eerie, spooky one, life hadn't been the same since it happened. The world's end.

Eleanor Hardy-Dearness (11)
Montgomery High School, Blackpool

Anne Boleyn

As she walked steadily up the steps, Queen Anne
knew in her heart that the crowd before her
didn't care that she was condemned. She had,
in fact, replaced their beloved, innocent Queen
Catherine on the throne, making the country
protestant in her stead.
Whoosh! Anne Boleyn was dead!

Amy Hughes (12)
Montgomery High School, Blackpool

The Trench

War was raging and I was in the muddy trenches.
The Germans were closing in. I was panicking,
sweating, holding my rifle. I knew I had to fight
but then air support came and bombed them.
I was saved. The word victory came up on the
screen of my Xbox.

Bradley Baldwin (12)
Montgomery High School, Blackpool

The Shining Star

Toby was flying in space and noticed the dazzling light in the sky. He flew closer to discover what it was. He dived past planets and stars while floating in the air. When he found the strange light, Toby Richards had discovered a meteorite! Millions of rocks falling, falling, falling.

Rebecca Macdonald (12)

Montgomery High School, Blackpool

The Graveyard

The graveyard was silent. The only noise was the noise of a raven, beckoning out to the dusk. Later, darkness tumbled in. Fog filled the cemetery. Echoes of loved ones deceased, hung around the graves. Then slowly, dawn crept in. The graveyard once again went into a solemn, dark silence.

Raven Finn (11)
Montgomery High School, Blackpool

Wanted Gnome-Snatcher

My favourite out of the collection had just been polished. My new, shiny gnome with his shiny, bright red button nose and tall, pointy, blue hat. He was out on the lawn when it happened. Suddenly the gnome-snatcher jumped out of the bushes then grabbed the gnome and ran!

Deniz Wynn (11)

Montgomery High School, Blackpool

The Adoption

After years of waiting they found her. Long, brown hair, beautiful, blue eyes and impeccable behaviour. They couldn't resist adopting her. Driving home, their family now complete. Eagerly waiting, a brother who they were sure would love her as much as they do. Tomorrow we get her a new collar.

Bethany McMillan (12)
Montgomery High School, Blackpool

The Robbery At A Beer Store

A random guy went into Bargain Booze to get some beer. When the man at the counter heavily over-priced the beer, the man realised there was a robbery. There was a robber under the desk so the robber stood up and pointed the gun at the counter man.

Daniel France (12)

Montgomery High School, Blackpool

Killer Penny

Bob was walking down the street. He was going into town and he stopped under Blackpool Tower to look at it. A boy on top of the tower dropped a penny by accident. It hit Bob on the head and he died. The little boy laughed.

Thomas Pilmore (11)
Montgomery High School, Blackpool

81

Street Race

John was walking down the street thinking what he was going to do with his life. He saw police storming a drug factory. *Would I make a good cop?* John thought. 'Nah!' he said aloud. He walked round the corner, saw a street racer storm round and said, 'Yes!'

Matthew Hickman (11)
Montgomery High School, Blackpool

Mystery Book

Tom and Kate saw a dirty, dusty trunk. As they opened it, they saw a book inside. When they opened the book itself, they both got sucked into a magical portal into a magical dinosaur, fairy land. 'Welcome,' said a fairy, 'your adventure has just begun!'
'What've we done?'

Catherine Elizabeth Walters (12)
Montgomery High School, Blackpool

Dark And Creepy Night

The field that I stood on lay beneath me like a green quilt as the bright lightning was blinding my eyes and the thunder deafening my ears. Suddenly it started raining while the earth began to shake and the scary wild animals surrounded my very spacious tent.

Jake Harrison (12)
Montgomery High School, Blackpool

My Dog

My dog is called Coco. She acts like a puppy even though she is a fully grown dog. When we try to bathe her she shakes and shakes and soaks Mum. It is so funny! Sometimes we end up chasing her around the back garden, but anyhow that's Coco.

Chloe Hulton (12)

Montgomery High School, Blackpool

The End Of The World

'Help!' I screamed, but nobody was there. The sun was gone. Suddenly the weather kicked in, everything was being blown around ruthlessly. The ground cracked and rumbled. A black hole appeared, dragging me in. I couldn't see. Then I was unconscious. When I woke I found I was only dreaming.

Lauren Hamilton-Shaw (11)

Montgomery High School, Blackpool

The Slums

As I was treading on the foul rubbish, I could see
dirty, poor children rummaging for food in the
junk. It was as if they were rubbish themselves.
It was such a shame. So I adopted one of them. I
once again gave a poor child a life worth living.

Ryan Townsley (12)
Montgomery High School, Blackpool

87

The Shadows From Hell

I was blinded by the darkness. I was deafened by a scream that shook the house all over. I froze. The hairs on the back of my neck stood on end. A trickle of sweat rolled down my spine. Then a dark figure erupted from the shadows from Hell …

Mia Prince (12)
Montgomery High School, Blackpool

The Wishing Star

The moon shone brightly and there was a cold chill in the air. The sky was as dark as ebony. The silver stars were twinkling above. As I gazed up a shooting star shot past, as far as the eye could see. That's when I made my very special wish …

Olivia Hamilton-Shaw (11)
Montgomery High School, Blackpool

The Wedding

Our family received an invitation to a special wedding. The search was on. I visited shop after shop, town after town, with no success. I had almost given up when quite by chance I saw it, shimmering in various shades of pink-perfection … the dress that was meant for me.

Danielle Woodhead (11)
Montgomery High School, Blackpool

Virtual What?

'Argh!' shouted the boy as his car blew up in flames. Everyone ran away whilst the emergency services were being called.
'Loser!' giggled the boy's friend. 'Too bad!' he said as he burst into laughter.
Then the Gran Turismo police arrived.
'Wanna play again?'
'Yeah, I'm in the Lamborghini.'

Hannah Carter (12)

Montgomery High School, Blackpool

The Horror Shop

Henry stared into the shop of horror. Horrified, Henry saw a man carving his knife through flesh and bones. Henry moved into the shop and the man waved his arms at Henry with blood and guts dripping down them. He spoke with a terrifying voice, 'You will be next, Henry.'

Hannah Munro (12)

Montgomery High School, Blackpool

Hannah And The Magic Star

Hannah marched around aimlessly, only to find a small star glowing on the jet-black floor. She edged closer and closer to it, the star dimming every second … as she touched it the star suddenly lit up. Both the star and Hannah shot up into the pure blue, starry sky.

Sophie Collier (12)
Montgomery High School, Blackpool

Jill And Jack

Jill and Jack went down the hill to collect a pail of water. Jill rolled up and fixed her crown and Jack came tumbling after. Then they fell in a ditch and met a witch who killed them and that's the end of the story for now. Poor Jack, Jill.

Sophie Bishop (11)

Montgomery High School, Blackpool

The Butchers

Once upon a time, not so long ago, there was a butcher. He sliced and diced, and he was the biggest killing machine in the whole town. Until one day a spirit of one of his pigs came back to haunt him. It said, 'One pound of sausages please.'

Christy Donnelly (12)
Montgomery High School, Blackpool

95

The Gleaming, Hungry Dolphin

The gleaming dolphin swam in the deep blue sea.
The dolphin got hungry, so he swam deeper into
the sea to hunt for some fish. He found some,
there were thousands. He dived for one and *snap*.
He caught one. He caught the tastiest fish ever.
He absolutely loved it.

Lauren Mudd (12)
Montgomery High School, Blackpool

A Day In The Life Of A Man!

He woke up one day feeling random. He got dressed in his irregular clothes, drank his deformed cup of coffee and set off to his random workplace in his weird car. His freaky job was being crazy. This is why he is most commonly called, 'The Amazing Random Man'!

Connor Magson (11)
Montgomery High School, Blackpool

97

The Dragon

'Freedom!' shouted Lancelot as he drove his sword through the dragon's scaly skin and pierced his heart. The dragon roared before it hit the hard ground. It shook the caves; it was about to collapse. He skidded out, he was safe. He ran home to his now safe village.

Matthew Sargent (11)

Montgomery High School, Blackpool

The Dream

The morning that Sophie finally decided to go
downstairs, her parents weren't happy. In fact
they looked almost explosive.
'Sophie Bishop, how dare you!'
She hung her head and just as she began to walk
upstairs, her alarm clock set off.
'Sophie, breakfast time!' shouted her mother …
Unexpectedly happy, surprisingly.

Taylor Wyles (12)
Montgomery High School, Blackpool

The Adventure Of Timmy The Donkey

Timmy galloped into the field in time to see
what the commotion was. In the middle stood
the giant! It collected every animal in it, including
Timmy.
The next day Timmy and his friends were on sale
at Montgomery's. Fiona bought him and kept him
in her pocket for school.

Fiona Hockey
Montgomery High School, Blackpool

The Storm

The storm started to approach the small village, people ran into their houses and jumped into their cars to escape to a different town. Billy had nowhere to go, he hid in an old garage when a lightning strike hit the window … He woke up in the garage.

James Osborne (11)
Montgomery High School, Blackpool

101

Humpty The Numpty

One day Humpty the Numpty was walking home
from school. He thought he would take a short
cut through the lonely field. When he got there
he saw a gang of bullies and they said to him,
'Give me your money or else!'
'No!'
So the bullies cracked his egg.

Dylan Cochrane (12)
Montgomery High School, Blackpool

The Blue Giant

The blue giant twisted and turned as it
desperately tried to escape. As it struggled it
became weaker and weaker. The poachers
drenched in bitter water as the whale slammed
his tail on the surface. The smooth-skinned animal
lay still as the water settled, poachers smiled at
their catch!

Sophie Reynolds (12)
Montgomery High School, Blackpool

Murder

Bob, just a normal man going to the paper shop.
As he was paying for what he was about to buy he
heard a scream. He ran out of the shop, maybe
for his life. He ran home.
Next thing he knew the murder was all over the
news!

Brandon Bostock (11)
Montgomery High School, Blackpool

The Snow

I walked across the cold and icy snow. Flakes fell heavily on my head … I saw Elli aim a ball of snow at me, so before I could bend down and get a handful of snow, my face was full of slushy ice. I tried to run but slid.

Mariesha Bryan (11)
Montgomery High School, Blackpool

The Storm

The storm was destroying the town. It was scary
for all of the citizens. The visibility was low,
people of the town were escaping. We got hit
really badly, many people were injured. By the
morning everything was fine, most people were
happy and all was fine until …

Jordon Hartley (12)
Montgomery High School, Blackpool

The Man That Deserved More

'Hey Bob,' said his wife.
'Hi,' said Bob.
'You okay, love?' questioned his wife.
'*No!*' shouted Bob.
'What's the matter?' asked his wife.
'Nothing, leave me alone,' shouted Bob.
'Sorry, love, I'm going out now, I'll be back later.'
When she came back Bob was dead, lying on the floor.

Lewis Christy (12)
Montgomery High School, Blackpool

The Creature

He entered the room, frightened to the bone and his skin white with terror. Then something stirred in the room and a tremendous growl came from a dark corner next to him. Suddenly a creature, with blood dripping from its large mouth, pounced onto him. Then came the unheard scream.

Charlotte Bird (11)

Montgomery High School, Blackpool

The Cannibal Hunter's Big Mistake

In the dark night a cannibal feasted on his food.
Flesh and blood was all over his hands and mouth
and there, lurking in the green bushes, was a
cannibal hunter. He aimed and fired. *Bang!* Then
he realised he had shot a dog who was eating
some raw steak.

Kyle Baxter (11)
Montgomery High School, Blackpool

Untitled

The kids went into the house. Tom went into the living room. Jack went into the kitchen. Chloe went into the bedroom. Suddenly a man with no face stabbed Chloe, Jack and then Tom. The children are still there, where they died. All their families died one week later.

Lloyd Hargreaves (12)

Rhyddings Business & Enterprise School, Accrington

Untitled

There was a boy wanting to be hard because he always got bullied in school. He trained hard and hard and didn't get anywhere.
One day he came upon this boy, they said he was quite hard. He protected him so he didn't have to worry ever again.

Zakir Khan (11)

Rhyddings Business & Enterprise School, Accrington

111

My First Date

He took me swiftly by the hand as we walked
along the river. Oh how handsome he was, all
muscly and sweet and smelt gorgeous. He took
me for some lovely tea and paid all the bill. He
walked me home, safe and sound, he came closer
and *kissed me!*

Shannon Marsland (11)
Rhyddings Business & Enterprise School, Accrington

My Prom Night

It was the prom, her eyes sparkled like the stars. Her dress was baby-pink and pearl-white. Her date was waiting downstairs for her. Her outfit was almost complete, a big, sparkly tiara completed her whole outfit. She walked out the door; tonight was the night …

Tonicha Bland (12)

Rhyddings Business & Enterprise School, Accrington

The Unknown Figure

I saw shadows of the misshapen branches outside,
I could hear leaves blowing through the slightly
open window. Suddenly floorboards began to
creak. I sat up as fast as a bullet from a gun.
The door flew open as I screamed. It remained
completely silent. Then he entered ...

Dee Haworth (12)
Rhyddings Business & Enterprise School, Accrington

The Spider King

In the dark, cold night me and my friends went into the forest. It was scary, I nearly fell over and my hands were as cold as ice. I found a dead spider in the mud and it wasn't looking good. Then the biggest spider in the world killed us all!

Joseph Shaw (12)

Rhyddings Business & Enterprise School, Accrington

What Have I Done?

It was a Sunday morning and I couldn't understand what had happened that Saturday night. Everything was a blur. I picked out the main parts I could remember. All I could remember was my friends pushing me to do something that I didn't want to do. To snog James!

Abbie Taylor (12)

Rhyddings Business & Enterprise School, Accrington

Unsatisfied Hunger

The eyeball glared at it. The one thing he had travelled all the way to town for, but as little Johnny stepped into the doorway of the doughnut shop, his appetite was soon shattered as his foot had landed in a gift a small dog had left this morning.

Malik Metcalfe (13)

Rhyddings Business & Enterprise School, Accrington

The Strange Happenings

As I was walking through a castle one day, I heard
a strange noise. Things started shaking, I turned
around and nothing was there. Things started
crashing, I could hear whining noises so I walked
towards the wardrobe where the noises were
coming from, and there it was, a ghost!

Katie Allonby (12)
Rhyddings Business & Enterprise School, Accrington

The Figure

I saw a dark figure. It came closer and closer and I was terrified. Maybe it was a shadow or someone looking for somebody to chase. I set off running into the cold, dark night sky but the figure came closer to me. All I could do was keep running.

Lucy Challoner (13)
Rhyddings Business & Enterprise School, Accrington

Hounds Of Hell

Its great red eyes, savage for blood, came running out of a sewer. I sprinted away. More screams were heard as people were torn apart. More dogs chased me, it was a fight for survival. Their blood-curdling howls drawing near. I swung round to see huge, death-bringing jaws.

Curt Boulderstone (13)

Rhyddings Business & Enterprise School, Accrington

Untitled

I walk into the scary house to find a dead rat, broken floorboards and ruined carpet. I scream as someone jumps from under the stairs. I am terrified as I find out it's an alien from Planet X. He takes me with him. Now Planet X is my home.

Jonathan Berry (14)
Rhyddings Business & Enterprise School, Accrington

Untitled

I was lying in bed, suddenly there was a crash. I
jumped up, what was it? I couldn't find anything.
There it went again, what if I was dreaming?
I knew I couldn't be, then I felt something or
someone move past me. A shiver went down my
spine ...

Ellis McNulty (15)
Rhyddings Business & Enterprise School, Accrington

The Return Of All Things

Thinking of all the things that had happened to me
over the past years, the weirdest was probably
on the X-15 station. I would like to tell you more
about that place but I can't because the X-15
station is the place where I died and came
back …

Matthew Kershaw (12)
Rhyddings Business & Enterprise School, Accrington

Untitled

I miss you every day; I miss you every night. I don't know what to do when I'm not with you. Just remember the good times we used to have, but now you have got married. You have had to move like a bird who has never returned.

Joshua Edmondson (13)
Rhyddings Business & Enterprise School, Accrington

The Lamb's Adventure

One day there lived a lamb and the lamb wandered out of the meadow. He kept wandering away until it got dark and the lamb got tired. He was going to go to sleep but suddenly he heard a gunshot. He ran very fast back to the meadow!

Anisha Khan (12)

Rhyddings Business & Enterprise School, Accrington

Untitled

It was Friday night at Mill Hill chippy. The queues were miles long. They were all queuing for fish and chips. Suddenly a fish came alive, all the people ran frantically around the town. I shouted for them to come back but the fish and chips started fighting.

Eric Morris (12)

Rhyddings Business & Enterprise School, Accrington

The Sunny Beach

Trotting along the hot, sandy beach with my beautiful white horse. The glittering sea sparkling in my eyes. The heat of the sun tickles my back. My horse, Sindy, gallops and makes the cool breeze hit me and rush through my golden hair. I fall off Sindy and awake.

Chelsie Singleton (13)

Rhyddings Business & Enterprise School, Accrington

127

Yelps And Squeals

You could hear his squeals and cries from inside. He was lonely and scared. He launched himself at the door, he yelped even more. He only got put outside because he was sick in Colleen's dinner and ripped up Conor's magazine. Poor Marley!

Rebecca Townsend (12)

St James' CE Sports College, Bolton

Untitled

I awoke in a misty mansion. Screeches and screams were approaching. My ammo was low. The dead but alive, bloodthirsty zombies that were in my view were stumbling towards me, but there was not just the one, there were hundreds and that's when I realised it was the end …

Nathan Dooner (13)

St James' CE Sports College, Bolton

What The Dark Can Do

I have to run, I have to leave. It might have been
a ghost, it might have been a trick of light, but
I had definitely seen something. My feet were
pounding on the wet grass, then darkness. I was
falling, that's when I saw it ... just floating, staring,
laughing ...

Oliver Shaw (13)

St James' CE Sports College, Bolton

Who?

That was the day. Yes, I thought my life would
end. The poison was there, right there in my
hand. I was just about to drink it when … *smash!*
Glass shattered everywhere. The poison was
spilt. Immediately terrified I asked, 'Who's there?'
All I heard was a cackle of laughter …

Thamina Akhtar (11)
St James' CE Sports College, Bolton

Haunted!

They both crept inside. 'Where is it?' Jessie
and Katie went looking for their ball in their
neighbour's garden. It was dusty everywhere.
'Hello, anyone there?' shouted Katie. There was
no reply.
Jessie went outside to look behind the shed. *Bang!*
She fell in a hole underground. She was gone …

Aimee Parmar (11)
St James' CE Sports College, Bolton

The Shadow

'What was that?' asked Milly cautiously.
'I don't know. Over there! A shadow, I saw a shadow,' screamed Charlotte.
As they crept along the dusty, wooden floorboards, there was a sudden *bang!* Milly tiptoed round the corner into the silent, dark and musty room. He stood there waiting menacingly …

Caitlin Sanders (11)
St James' CE Sports College, Bolton

133

Stuck!

Darkness crept upon me, numbing my limp arms and legs. Where was I? My uncontrollable eyes scanned the room. I tried to move but my body didn't allow me to! I was stuck! Suddenly, light! Bright light flooded the empty space. A shadowed figure loomed in the doorway …
'No! He's back!'

Khadija Iqbal (12)
St James' CE Sports College, Bolton

Birthday Surprise

I stood outside waiting. It was quiet, too quiet.
Suddenly I heard a noise come from inside the
house. What was it? I walked inside slowly. It was
pitch-black. I opened the door, it creaked …
'Surprise!'
Then someone shouted out excitedly, 'Happy
birthday, Amy!'
I giggled. Balloons burst loudly.

Lydia Bancks (13)
St James' CE Sports College, Bolton

Black Shadow

As I went to get the bin bags from the cellar,
I walked down the steep stairs. I grabbed the
bags. Suddenly I saw a black shadow. It growled!
I stepped back and slipped. I banged my head and
the lights came on. It was ... *argh!* Dog!

Lorenzo Soruri (13)
St James' CE Sports College, Bolton

Run, Lance, Run

I just took up my position, waiting for that special time. I examined my opponents, two English, a French guy and two Americans. My heart was pumping and these words repeating in my head: *this is my time now.* The adrenaline rushed through my small body. Everything blurry, then *bang!*

Caine Jackson (13)

St James' CE Sports College, Bolton

Firstborn

There she was, looking right at me! I didn't know
how to help. Do I run? Stay? Scream? It happened.
I was prepared, but obviously not enough.
'I'm scared,' she said worryingly. Then she
screamed so loud, it burst my eardrums.
'Here's your baby. Congratulations!' said the
midwife proudly.

Kristina Kelleway (13)
St James' CE Sports College, Bolton

Beast

The taste of blood was sweet against Victor's tongue. He had been in battle on the Mourning Plains for two years.
'Victor!'
Once the beast, Victor, heard his name, he turned around out of instinct. He thought to himself, *am I Victor?* In his blindness, Victor was struck down dead.

Nathan Jariwala (12)
St James' CE Sports College, Bolton

Little Lion Cub In Danger

The poor, little, innocent lion cub looked up with
watery eyes. Surrounded by angry men with guns,
he had nowhere to go. The men then shouted,
'1, 2, 3!' and shut the lion cub in a wooden box.
What can the little lion cub do? He can't get away.

Sophie Eastwood (12)
St James' CE Sports College, Bolton

Three Ninjas Kick Back

Three teenagers learn karate as well as baseball.
They go to China to help their grandad because
he's in danger. They save their grandad, make
a new friend called Kabaya, win karate contest.
They get home for their important baseball game,
they win the game with help from their new
friend.

Burnden Horrocks (11)

St James' CE Sports College, Bolton

141

Charlie's Adventure

Charlie, a young boy, and family were poor. He lived near a mysterious chocolate factory. He had no chance of getting a Golden Ticket, but one day, Charlie found one! Charlie visited the chocolate factory. His luck was in, in the factory he had a fabulous time.
Charlie's Chocolate Factory.

Charlie Murphy (11)
St James' CE Sports College, Bolton

The Mission

David has a very dangerous mission to complete. He has to move quickly or he'll get blown to bits. Dr Gauge has set a very powerful bomb in London. David has a lot of pressure on him to disarm it. However, he is successful.

Dhylan Jadwa (11)
St James' CE Sports College, Bolton

143

Lonely Bones

The abandoned and starving child sits in the corner of the narrow hallway, not talking, but just sitting rocking and staring at this one place. She's petrified and helpless.
A man called Dylan finds her and helps her get through her worthless life. The girl builds hope.

Alicia Pryzsieniak (11)
St James' CE Sports College, Bolton

Attacked

Here we were, me and the monster, in the middle of nowhere. He was extremely hungry and I was so scared I couldn't move. He stared back at me with fiery red eyes and then, as fast as lightning, lunged himself at me. I ran and didn't stop …

Rebecca Preston (11)
St James' CE Sports College, Bolton

The Magnificent Iz!

It was Monday and Izzy went to school.
At home she loved to write a story about her as a
powerful girl who was very popular.
One day she accidentally sent it to her friend who
printed it off! Then Izzy became famous and her
life changed forever!

Amy Carter (11)
St James' CE Sports College, Bolton

The Survivor

His heart was pounding. Adrenaline pumped
through his veins. Would he make it? They were
getting closer. He quickly turned round and fired
a few bullets at the crowd following. He ran to his
front door, yanked it open and ran in. Safe at last.

Alex Phillips (11)
St James' CE Sports College, Bolton

147

The Secret Garden

Mary is a spoilt, bratty, selfish girl. Her mum and dad die so she moves to her hunchback uncle's mansion. She makes friends with Dicken. Her attitude becomes more friendly and kind. While playing in the gardens, Mary finds a secret garden. It is the most beautiful garden ever.

Prinal Vegad (11)

St James' CE Sports College, Bolton

The Boy, The Palace And The Bomb

Billy had to get inside. He told his sidekick to distract the guards, then he ran inside. It was beautiful. 'Too bad I have to blow this place up.' He lay down the bomb and armed it, then he made his escape into the old, rusty helicopter.

Ben Atherton (11)
St James' CE Sports College, Bolton

Imagine

There's another world with extraordinary creatures. Men, women and children have tails, they are also blue. I enter this mind-blowing machine which takes me to that dimension. However, the army wants to destroy this world and they want me to do it because I have gained their trust.

Rudra Dave (12)

St James' CE Sports College, Bolton

Untitled

Before I could interrupt, Susan stopped and with
a zombie-like face, pointed to the shadowed sky.
My jaw dropped as I followed her lead and gasped
in astonishment! Screams echoed throughout the
city's centre and birds scattered as the saucer-like
aircraft blocked out all signs of light …

James Wardle (12)
St James' CE Sports College, Bolton

Bang! What Is It?

Bang! The door slammed. It was there! I scuttled across the dining room floor. It leaped onto the sideboard, then knocked the jar of maggots over. I screamed. Then it made a squeaking sound. A dozen came out, knocked me over and …
My life flashed before my eyes …

Sophia Hall (11)
St James' CE Sports College, Bolton

Untitled

'*Run!*' screamed Jack.
The policemen were chasing them through town.
'Quick, round this corner,' whispered Sam.
'Phew, that was a close one. I can't believe we got
away from them.'
They heard a policeman calling for back-up. He
spotted them. 'Oi, you two, you're nicked!' he
shouted.

Sam Willber (12)
St James' CE Sports College, Bolton

The Rabbit's Retreat

Little white rabbit, running through sharp, thorny, prickly bushes as the eagle is swooping down. The rabbit is doomed, it's about to strike! But the rabbit jumps into its nice, cosy hole where it can survive one more day.

Kynan Fleming (12)
St James' CE Sports College, Bolton

Am I In Space?

I stumbled in the dark, gloomy, scary house. *Bang!*
Was I in the right house? Suddenly, someone came
down and looked like gruesome green bogies!
This old, cranky, cruel guy cried out, *'Biaasgh!'*
Was I in space or Britain? This guy came near me!
'Stop! Stop!' I cried. 'Noooo!'

Yameen Mallu (11)
St James' CE Sports College, Bolton

155

Candy Wars

In a candy galaxy far, far away, there was a large candy ball called the Death Star. Lollipop Luke clashed his gummy saber with the Darth Decayer's. Lollipop Luke crashed him to the ground, his evil body shaking. 'Wait!' he said. 'I am your father …'
'Noooo!' replied Lollipop Luke.

Zain Ahmed (11)
St James' CE Sports College, Bolton

On The Move

Speeding swiftly, rapidly and anxiously down the lane. Approaching Syndey at an extremely fast pace was a man Syndey didn't know. Suddenly the traffic lights turned red. Syndey was trembling. What would she do? The man came to the car and asked, 'Have you got your driving licence?'

Zain Hussain (12)

St James' CE Sports College, Bolton

157

The Wow Match

In a blink of an eye, pass after pass, shot after shot, goal after goal. It's nerve-racking. The Champions League final. Full time penalties. First one in, second one, third and fourth. If they score they will win the trophy, but does he score? Of course not! *Boo!*

Callum Hughes (12)

St James' CE Sports College, Bolton

The Runaway

He walked in. Terrified as he was, he opened
the case, took one and left. Wondering what
happened, people started to question him. He ran
home as fast as a cheetah, but he didn't make it
… Turning the corner at the speed of light, he fell.
Hurt! Blood everywhere.

Alexandra Green (11)
St James' CE Sports College, Bolton

Wasteland

One man and his dog strutting through the wasteland, wary of the oncoming danger. They approach a good friend. *Bark!* The dog is barking at an unknown figure. *Whoosh!* The man flies into the air, propelled by a rope. Night falls, they come. The man and his dog are gone.

Benjamin Toovey (12)

St James' CE Sports College, Bolton

Tick

Tick, tick, tick. It gets ready to pop. We cannot move. We are too enticed. It is still going. Five, four, three, two, one. *Cuckoo! Cuckoo!*
'Dinner, children!' Mum shouts through the house.
We all fly in, shaking like the quivering plates of jelly on the side for dessert.

Luke Thurston (12)
St James' CE Sports College, Bolton

Baseball

Jim was running, running for his life. He was hurting all over. If he stopped he would never live it down. He had no choice, he had to jump for it …
What a catch! He had caught the ball. The Blues had won the trophy! Another great game!

Jake Knight (11)
St James' CE Sports College, Bolton

The Rush

Time was running out. Jenny ran through the mammoth town breathing deeply. She wondered if she was gonna do it. Three minutes left. She ran faster and faster! She finally reached the library.
'Can I return this book?'
'Yes,' said the librarian, 'you are just in time.'
Phew, thought Jenny.

Alisha Patel (12)
St James' CE Sports College, Bolton

163

Odd Family

A posh man and his family live over the road.
They are total weirdos. Soon I can see red,
glowing knife marks on the floor. I am eager
to find out what is going on. I sense fear in his
family's eyes. My fingers are eager for 999!

Daniel Alogba (11)
St James' CE Sports College, Bolton

Lost

Kimbley entered the murky room. It echoed with the sounds of dripping water. *Drip, drip!* Bitter winds sent shivers up her spine. Suddenly creepy, luminous eyes darted at her. What was it? Goosebumps covered her clammy skin. Nervously she called her parents. Her voice rebounded. Nobody could hear her voice …

Khairun Nisa Ali (12)
St James' CE Sports College, Bolton

Heart Pounding

Sarah's heart pounded like a beating drum, she thought her whole life had ended. She'd only been on a family day out. The car zoomed along, as a lion that had escaped chased them. *Whoosh!* They found an exit. They darted towards it at 100 miles per hour. Safe!

Georgia Clarke (12)

St James' CE Sports College, Bolton

Little Red Riding Hood

Little Red Riding Hood took muffins to her grandmother's. When she was in the forest she saw a wolf. When she got to her grandmother's, she wondered why she looked so weird. An axeman saw the wolf trying to eat her. He knocked down the door and killed the wolf.

Katie Harper (12)
St James' CE Sports College, Bolton

Forgot

Simon woke up, put on his clothes, then set out
for work. 'Oh no, Pants!' So he went back, put
on his pants, set out, came back, locked the door
and set off for work. 'Oh man, I'm gonna be late.'
'Hey Simon, weren't you going on holiday?'

Junior Conceicao (12)
St James' CE Sports College, Bolton

Haunted!

Timmy walked into the house, but what he didn't
know was that it was haunted! It was late at night.
Timmy walked down the corridor and suddenly,
he heard a door creak open …
He was so scared, he ran out of the door and
never ever returned!

Mark Fisher (12)
St James' CE Sports College, Bolton

Secret Boy ...

Lucy met him in the forest. She had seen him
before in her dreams. Why was he here? He
walked towards her and held her hand. She felt
his coldness like stone.
'Hello Lucy,' he said with a laugh behind it.
'Hello,' she murmured quietly.
'I am a vampire.'

Niamh White (11)
St James' CE Sports College, Bolton

Humpty Goes Rock Climbing

There was once an egg called Humpty. One day
he went rock climbing on Table Mountain. He had
to get to the top to beat his record of one hour.
But then his foot slipped and he was hanging on
for dear life. He cried, 'Help!'
Splat! Just some runny egg …

Ryan Aldred (11)
St James' CE Sports College, Bolton

It!

Looking around, he shivered. Billy was alone in the dark. Bushes rustled, trees shook. What was it? Who was it? It was making him dizzy. Rustling in every direction. Which direction was it going to come from? The rustling got louder. *Bang!* Out it came. But what happened to Billy?

Matthew Beswick (12)

St James' CE Sports College, Bolton

Bullet

The bullet made a sudden dart. She then let the gun escape her clutches. It slipped through her bloodstained hands. She looked at the astonishing scene which lay before her …
In the scarlet puddle lay Evermore. 'What have I done?' A series of questions rushed through her. Death appeared …

Kajal Ladva (13)
St James' CE Sports College, Bolton

173

The Unexpected Encounter

Grace walked up the crooked stairs, back against the wall, sweaty palms clutching the banister for dear life. She saw blood splattered on the bathroom floor. Out of the corner of her eye, she saw Naomi's charm bracelet on the bedpost. She entered. Naomi's body was on the floor …

Elizabeth Gannon (12)
St James' CE Sports College, Bolton

Der Riese

Four people, one haunted mansion flooded with gruesome dead or alive zombies. Our ammo was low and more and more were howling and screaming from a distance. Then the dreaded Imperial Army charged at us as we used our last bit of water to quench our thirst ... it ended!

Adam Green (13)
St James' CE Sports College, Bolton

The Race For Life

Matt was running for his life. He had just borne witness to the most bloodthirsty murder. He could feel the cold breath of the killer on the back of his neck. Suddenly, two muscular arms wrapped around his throat and he was pulled to the ground. Death was upon him …

Nathan Byrne (13)
St James' CE Sports College, Bolton

Capture

Paul was in danger! Being held hostage by two African pirates. The boat was rocking fiercely as the waves were crashing against the rocks. His only option was to swim for his life. He jumped out of the boat and started to swim to land. He was safe at last!

Emma McFarland (12)

St James' CE Sports College, Bolton

177

Break Time

I was running, a flat-out sprint. But he was
gaining. I weaved to the side as his hand whistled
through the air. The wall - I had to reach it.
I managed. I jumped and spun to face his
disgruntled expression.
'Best game of tig - ever!'

Bethany Lythgoe (12)
St James' CE Sports College, Bolton

Who's There?

I was home alone and there was a knock at the door. I didn't answer. They knocked again, so I stayed still. They looked through the window. I dived and hid under the table, my heart racing. Then the phone rang. It was my mum saying, 'Let me in!'

Grace Molloy (13)
St James' CE Sports College, Bolton

The Story Of Cinderella

Cinderella, lovely girl. *Boom!* Her world came crashing down. She was left with no one but her stepmother. She was invited to the royal ball. Then her fairy godmother appeared. She found the man of her dreams. He tried to find her. He did and they lived happily ever after!

Kate Hilton (12)

St James' CE Sports College, Bolton

Harry Potter And The Half-Blood Prince: Into The Rushes

Harry and Ginny stood in the burrow with their backs to a window. A sudden flash! They turned to see fire dancing around them. In a second, they knew why. Bellatrix Lestrange appeared. He and Ginny ran after her but she disappeared and they turned, the burrow was burning down …

Lewie Parkinson-Jones (12)

St James' CE Sports College, Bolton

Baby Annabelle

Annabelle haunts her in her sleep. With a gleam in her eye and ragged dress, some would mistake her for a ghost.
She fell onto the floor, *thud!* Daisy woke up …
'Annabelle? I had forgotten about you. In the morning we'll buy you a new dress … my baby Annabelle!'

Bethan Stacey (12)
St James' CE Sports College, Bolton

Last Minutes

Michael sprinted for dear life. The high-pitched, evil cackle of the man who attempted to slaughter him haunted his ears. His cold breath could be felt on his neck. *Thud!* Michael fell in a heap on the bloody floor with an axe in his head. He moved no more.

Saaif Umerji (13)
St James' CE Sports College, Bolton

183

The Lonely Tennis Ball

Waiting … still waiting, when are they going to come? All the fun times I had with them, I could feel that fast, fresh feeling of the wind whizzing past me! I hope they don't leave me here! I'm only a green tennis ball, but it's not over, there's still more …

Kezar Vanat (13)

St James' CE Sports College, Bolton

The Destroyer

It tears the face off, arms and legs litter the
floor. An evil grin appears on my face. They are
damaged beyond repair. I have eradicated them!
'Billy, don't give your sister's dolls to the dog!'
Mum yells …
And the grin is wiped off my face.

Lisa Norcross (12)
St James' CE Sports College, Bolton

185

Mr Bean Stories: 3

'Huh-err, huh-err,' as he panted out of breath. 'You come here and get a load of my fist,' the Japanese screamed in half a second. Mr Bean got to a dead end. Soon the Japanese arrived with their scrunched up faces. *Dundunderrr!* 'Hayaa! Kapow! Fadoom!' He won!

Aadesh Patel (12)
St James' CE Sports College, Bolton

John Pushed ...

John pushed the door open. The old hinges creaked as the door opened. John slowly crept inside. The light flickered and the floorboards creaked. In the corner there was a cabinet. John crept over to it. The cabinet was covered in dust. On the cabinet was the diamond …

Michael Hart (12)
St James' CE Sports College, Bolton

187

Alice In Wonderland

'Will you marry me?'
'Ah! No! What? A rabbit in clothes?' Following
it to a hole, Alice fell down. Found herself in a
wonderful world with old friends, from red to
white queen. Alice became a champion to the
white queen to slay the Jabberwocky.
'Will you marry me?'
'No!'

Helen Jackson (12)
St James' CE Sports College, Bolton

Bob's Shopping Death

Bob went to the shop, he died. Everyone was
shocked. His funeral was sad, everyone missed
him. But soon they would be with him because
an assassin called Ezio, and his team, came to the
funeral, undercover, and murdered them all!

Dominic Gannon (12)

St James' CE Sports College, Bolton

Avatar

Tall, blue and magical. Small, tanned and mysterious. For the first time Stephen felt what it was like to be his own avatar. Wonderful mysteries lay deep in the jungle of Hakatowa. A hidden world that no other human knew about. But then sudden death happens in Hakatowa …

Courtney Dunwell (12)
St James' CE Sports College, Bolton

Untitled

Viola pretended to be her older brother,
Sebastian, to enter the football team, Illeria.
Viola found it hard to fit in with his bad-boy
roommates. Her fantastic moves and unbelievable
skill, no one could get past her. A disaster
struck when the real Sebastian came home and
everything went
wrong …

Amy Hennefer (12)
St James' CE Sports College, Bolton

191

Vampiric Encounters

Tom ran. The presence of the vampire all around him, the stench of death looming in the school corridor. His friend dead, lying in a pool of blood. A high-pitched squeak rang throughout the building as Tom tripped on the bloody floor. The vampire stood over him, smiling scarily …

Daniel Kearns (13)

St James' CE Sports College, Bolton

Evolution!

Evolution! Putting the agility and speed into the
car. Making the fastest car in the world. Putting
extra time to making the gears good. Shaping the
car into a new shape. Getting the right attitude
and adjustment. Going the extra mile. It is the
immense car, fast and furious.

Tayyib Abbas (11)
St James' CE Sports College, Bolton

193

The Non-Stop Windy Road Of Fire

We were stuck. We took a right, we took a left.
'It's no use. Where should we go?'
Just then huge flaming balls (that looked like
meteorites) shot from every corner. Then a huge
figure stood on the car … but they did not die.
Then a voice cackled! They'd disappeared!

Aadil Adia (11)

St James' CE Sports College, Bolton

194

The Lonely Baked Bean

Left all alone. Dark. The poor bean had been
abandoned and forgotten about. Drowning in
his own juice, Billy Bean had to survive. As he
clambered up to the peak of the tin, Billy Bean
could not see his friends. Microwaved! His friends
had been baked alive! Left all alone!

Tia Sherrington (13)
St James' CE Sports College, Bolton

195

Eve!

Screeching noises came from a minute building.
She walked closer. *Bang!* The door opened,
shaking the entire building. She entered the dark
room. Bats flew everywhere. Gigantic spiders
with scissors as legs came towards her. The lights
were on!
'Well?'
'A cut, wash and blow,' said Eve to the
hairdresser.

Emily Craven (12)
St James' CE Sports College, Bolton

The Haunted House

'Come on, don't be a baby,' joked Becky.
'Fine, I'll come, but if anything happens to me,
you're responsible,' Amy shouted.
Becky and Amy walked up the bumpy road to the
haunted house and opened the door. *Creak!* They
walked inside. *'Argh! Help!'* shouted the girls.
Bang! The door locked …

Rachel Kirby (11)
St James' CE Sports College, Bolton

Dodged

It swerved, slid and darted as the car tried to escape the police. Now the police were really catching up to the robber. As the robber began to pick up speed, *crash!* The robber looked behind him, relieved. The police car had crashed. He sped up and surely escaped.

Niall Airey (12)

St James' CE Sports College, Bolton

Salty Water

I could feel the wind rush through my hair. I felt
the salty water in my breath. The water rushed
through my toes. Was this the end? Suddenly I
started drifting in the air … how was I doing this?
It couldn't be, or could it?
I was an angel!

Holly McKewan (11)
St James' CE Sports College, Bolton

Lord Of The Rings

Legolas fires an arrow and hits the Orc, he falls off and Aragon runs. Gimley throws an axe and hits the archer straight off a cliff, straight to the ground. Legolas gets on a horse and goes to Blacksorrows. Gimley is last there and Legolas runs to help Aragon.

Samuel Liptrot (11)

St James' CE Sports College, Bolton

The Sarah Jane Adventures

Sarah went to her attic. She asked Mr Smith, 'Is there any breaking news yet?'
Mr Smith replied, 'Yes, there is a meteor coming to Earth and it's by the trickster.'
When she went outside, the trickster kidnapped her. Will she be able to save Earth?

Manisha Sitpura (11)

St James' CE Sports College, Bolton

Matilda

Matilda was a brave kid who liked to read. She was adopted when she was a baby. She had dark brown hair like chocolate and light blue eyes. At school, Matilda's teacher was called Mrs Honey. She was really kind and the wicked head teacher, Mrs Trunchball, was cruel.

Riya John (12)
St James' CE Sports College, Bolton

202

Badboy Crew

'Ouch! Stop it!'
Billy could see the boys of Badboy Crew torturing
the little boy. He ran to his friends. 'Can you help
me stop The Badboy Crew torturing the little kid
there?'
'Are you mad? We'll get tortured.'
So he went on his own and ended up in hospital.

Muhammed Atcha (11)
St James' CE Sports College, Bolton

Shadowed!

Alone with no father, friend and one mother. I wondered if life could get any worse. Yesterday I dreamt of a shadow staring at me. Gradually, this dream became reality.
Now the shadow follows me everywhere I go. We've been together so long, my fear of shadows has been conquered.

Pritika Patel (13)
St James' CE Sports College, Bolton

The Axeman

Big, strong, bearded man came up with a huge
axe, striking down and claiming another set of
work done. I tried to escape, too late.
'Well boy, what do you want?' he said.
'One Christmas tree,' I replied nervously.
It was like he wanted to cut me in two. Weirdo.

Kane Fitzharris (12)
St James' CE Sports College, Bolton

The Chase!

I tripped and fell as I ran down the street. My heart was racing as I lay there, hoping I wouldn't be seen. Cowering in the corner, I heard a voice,
'Nikkie, Nikkie.'
How did he know my name?
'Nikkie, Nikkie!'
A shadow emerged from the darkness.
'Tag! You're it!'

Elizabeth Turner (13)
St James' CE Sports College, Bolton

Mysterious House

I went to the mysterious house. The windows were boarded up and there was never anyone there. The garden was beautiful as ever. I went into the dark house. There were pictures on the walls and flies everywhere. I looked all over the house …
There he was!

Georgia Ithell (12)
St James' CE Sports College, Bolton

207

Trick Or Tree?

Lucy finds a door in her new house. She walks
through. *Bang!* It closes. Lucy begins to walk
backwards as she notices a light coming towards
her. *Bump!* A talking tree! They make friends.
They meet a bear, they get chased by the bear,
they get eaten by the bear!

Rhianne Greer (12)
St James' CE Sports College, Bolton

It Was An Accident

Daniel crept down behind the wall as the black figures looked in his direction, holding his breath, silence. The smallest figure mumbled something to his partner as they both stumbled off. Daniel opened his eyes after another dream about the biggest prank he regrets he did.

Rebecca Russell (12)

St James' CE Sports College, Bolton

The Cannibal

The body is on the floor, blood everywhere. I, Jamie Shepherd, am a murder detective. I look around and there seems to be a blood trail. I follow this dark, thick blood outside. I see it! A person with blood in his mouth, stained teeth. This is the infamous cannibal.

Jamie Shepherd (12)
St James' CE Sports College, Bolton

Blood! Murder!

He was walking down a dark, deserted back
street, alone. Suddenly he heard a sound! 'Argh!'
screamed something.
Simon froze. Silence! Blood! Simon was petrified.
He could hear rustling sounds in the bushes.
Someone came out. Simon closed his eyes.
'Simon! Wake up!'
He realised it was all a dream.

Masood Azhar Rawat (13)
St James' CE Sports College, Bolton

Saturday Night Nightmare

Bang! The bullet goes straight into the murderer's heart. Blood everywhere. People are hiding with terror, everyone screaming! Harry is shaking, holding the gun, while the murderer is on the floor, blue in the face and covered with blood all over.

'That film was good, Sarah!'

'Hmmm.'

Chloe Tonge (12)

St James' CE Sports College, Bolton

Breathless

She fell into the darkness. So quiet and so all alone, Ellie was kneeling at her grandmother's grave, mourning with sorrow. The night was dark and rain drenched her from head to toe. Suddenly a hand grabbed her mouth, the grip getting tighter and tighter. Gasping for breath, she fainted.

Heshini Nimthara Gunasekara (12)
St James' CE Sports College, Bolton

The Shadows

Eerie shadows lingered at every turn; an inexplicable twilight hung over the town. Somewhere overhead a street light flickered. Nervously, I quickened my pace, my heartbeat thundering. I slid discreetly down a street, ran into my house, slammed on the lights. A pair of eyes narrowed ...
'You're late, Faye.'

Joely Randle (12)
St James' CE Sports College, Bolton

The Search

Gasping for breath, Tom sped around the room. Sweat appeared on his forehead. *Where is it?* he thought. Footsteps were heard in the background. Salty tears ran down his cheeks and he grieved. Tom froze. He could feel breath on his neck.

'Found your homework yet, son?' asked his father.

Meera Sonara (12)

St James' CE Sports College, Bolton

The Cold Winter's Day

Very cold winter's day, no one in sight, all alone
in the park. No light. A man stood like a tree,
watching the young girl walk past. Running fast,
the girl was dead. Rushing, rapid, red blood
everywhere …

Megan Kelly (13)
St James' CE Sports College, Bolton

The Wait

I sat there waiting in the dark, wondering when it would next see me. Distinct screams came from the distance, echoing. My heart started pounding as I squirmed in my seat. *Thud! Thud! Thud!* Someone was coming! *Thud! Thud! Thud!* It got louder and louder, then there was silence …

Jakub Thornley (13)
St James' CE Sports College, Bolton

Secrets, Secrets And More Secrets

Two young girls who were completely different - one inspired by Anne Frank, the other just trampy. India and Kitty just met up after India ran away from home. India's parents were shocked while India was hiding in the attic. After appearing on the news, India went back home.

Jessica Ruda (13)
St James' CE Sports College, Bolton

Untitled

He approached the bed, silently creeping like a spider. Silent like a mouse. *Drip, drip, drip,* the liquid on his body dropped like rain. Rubble fell from his hands like the ones of a destruction man.
'George, you're late! You've been doing extra work, hmm?'
'Yes, I have been love.'

Liam Brooks (13)
St James' CE Sports College, Bolton

219

Little Red Riding Hamster

Little Red Riding Hamster made her way through the woods to Granny's house. As she knocked on the door, she heard something. She knocked frantically just as a squirrel jumped out of a bush wielding a knife! Red squealed as she saw her reflection in the end of the blade …

Apple Elliott (13)

St James' CE Sports College, Bolton

Finding Nemo

Nemo is taken by a human, when he goes past 'the drop off'. His dad goes to look for him and makes friends with Dory on the way, who loses her memory. They have to face numerous challenges to find Nemo! When they finally do, they become a closer family.

Chloe Stott (13)

St James' CE Sports College, Bolton

Born To Run

Patrick took his normal walk along the canal. *Yelp!*
A noise came from the canal. Patrick and Best
Mate loved playing fetch on the park.
'Come here, boy!'
Best Mate had gone forever!
'Three, two, one, go!' Brighteyes was running for
his life! He ran with speed, power and agility!

Ben Timmis (12)
St James' CE Sports College, Bolton

The Man Immortal

The man stood inside the back street only wearing a long, black cloak. Neon lights flickered above grey storm clouds, closing in on the man. A face appeared on the cloud, pedestrians oblivious to the oncoming blackout. The man hurled himself at the skies, never to be seen again, ever.

Krishna Chauhan (13)
St James' CE Sports College, Bolton

223

Hunter, Survivor, Prey

No one can hear you scream in space …
One man alone on a distant planet, an unknown
enemy lurks in the darkness, expanding its hunting
ground. His ammo counter flashing low, a hiss
from the darkness and then a terrifying scream.
The two species are not alone. What's out there?

Sean Mooney (13)
St James' CE Sports College, Bolton

The Mystery Shadow

She saw a dark shadow in the corner of her eye, approaching her from behind. What was it? She slowly turned around to see what was following her. No one was there! She started trembling with fear, not knowing what to expect. She quickly ran back. Luckily, she's now safe.

Bethany Holt (12)
St James' CE Sports College, Bolton

225

Prom Queen Battles

The new girl, who does she think she is? Just because her eyes are beautifully bright and blue and her hair sweeps the floor. So what? She's still not going to get my crown! I will be prom queen. I've earned it. That crown will be mine and mine only.

Walinase-Chiuta Chisenga (12)
St James' CE Sports College, Bolton

Pop

I was waiting, I was ready to pop. In fact I was desperate. All I was waiting for was the little jingle that triggered my go, then I leapt, turned and popped out of my box and … *pop* goes the weasel!

Amy Deveney (13)
St James' CE Sports College, Bolton

War 4 Home

The vast, empty and deserted wasteland. Stepped
out from the safety of my home. The war of alien
against the human race was over. Then something
dashed by … *snap!* A twig broke, something came
out. *Alien!* I thought to myself, but then it said,
'Come here kid, we've won!'

Mubin Chachia (12)
St James' CE Sports College, Bolton

228

Your Turn ...

She stood and waited for the man to say, 'It's your turn.' Her stomach was turning and her head felt dizzy. Was she really going to go through with this again? She thought to herself, *come on, Lola*. The man said it was her turn for the big dipper!

Amelia Wrennall (13)
St James' CE Sports College, Bolton

Dream

Megan had a dream, a fabulous dream. She walked to school and sang and danced all the way. A poster appeared saying, *Are You The Dancer?* Her dream was half beaten. Her dream came true. She was a dancer for the universe, a singer too. Her dream became a career.

Nicole Jackson (13)

St James' CE Sports College, Bolton

Disappearance

One day, Sarah and her family went to the
beach. The sand was gold and the sea was clear
blue. After that, they went for a walk on the
cliffs. Sarah's sisters ran ahead. When the rest
of the family got to the top of the hill, they had
disappeared …

Olivia Mills (11)

St James' CE Sports College, Bolton

A Wonder

He grabbed the rusty door handle and stepped through the door with a shiver through his bones. The big, open staircase looked tattered and rotten, all the walls covered in slime and cobwebs.
Suddenly, he heard noises coming from upstairs - voices and screeching, then a dark shadow appeared slowly …

Jessica Scott (12)

West Craven High Technology College, Barnoldswick

Emma's Gone!

I went up to the eerie house, vermin decaying in the yard. Emma dared me to knock on the door. Before I got there, a stinking old lady came out. I looked back at Emma, she had gone! The old woman cackled, 'Is there any wonder?' What did she mean?

Sophie Metcalfe (12)

West Craven High Technology College, Barnoldswick

Kidnapped

As she was walking down the street, she came past a mysterious house and heard a scream. She went to check it out. The walls were covered in slime and as she stepped in, a man came out of nowhere. She screamed, but he grabbed her and ran off …

Marianne White (13)
West Craven High Technology College, Barnoldswick

The Stalker

Sprinting the fastest I could, the eerie man was
still catching up to me. I felt like I was going to
choke on my tongue. I could hardly breathe. I had
a bead of sweat dribbling down past my eyebrow.
This man wasn't just a stalker, he was deadly,
murderous …

Chloe Bickerdyke (13)
West Craven High Technology College, Barnoldswick

Please Help Me!

Yesterday I was walking home and my grandma saw me. She was happy. But then I realised somebody was following me. But who? I was scared. Then suddenly, I realised - this is not my street, this place isn't even real. But then I got stabbed. Who though?

Hollie Browne (12)

West Craven High Technology College, Barnoldswick

Untitled

I died four years ago by getting pushed off a cliff
by my worst enemy. So now it's time to go and
give her some payback!
I got dressed and made myself visible. 'I'll wait
until she walks past the canal and push her in. She
will drown.'

Chloe Standen (12)
West Craven High Technology College, Barnoldswick

Unexpected

I died a year ago today. I was only 13. But you're wondering how I died? It was a cold, dark night, I was walking home. This teenager was following me and yelling stuff. I got scared and ran. I found a place to hide and *bang!* He shot me.

Courtney Hartley (13)

West Craven High Technology College, Barnoldswick

The Shadow

I died a year ago today. This is how I died: I got chased by a shadowy, dark creature. I ran through the wheat field and over the bridge. I thought the shadowy, dark figure had gone, but it hadn't. Then it grabbed me and threw me into the canal …

Danielle Wellock (13)

West Craven High Technology College, Barnoldswick

The Last Walk

The gate was rusty and the garden was a wreck. It was full of brambles and poison ivy. I opened the gate and walked slowly up the slimy, muddy path to the rotten house. I could smell must and dampness already. I clutched the door handle nervously and …

Sarah McGuiness (13)

West Craven High Technology College, Barnoldswick

The House Down The Road

The house was deformed and very damp. We thought it was haunted. We were correct. Mrs Crocker was the local witch, or so we imagined. She lived in this slanted home. It had obviously been vandalised before and never fixed. Then we saw headlights. We peddled fast. We returned …

Bethany Wood (13)

West Craven High Technology College, Barnoldswick

Axe Man

One murderous night, I was on my way home.
But when I was walking, I froze. I halted, twisted
round and saw a deadly man holding an axe. I
screamed and sprinted. He sprinted. When I
turned round, he was gone! I turned back … he
was in front of me!

Natasha Porter (13)

West Craven High Technology College, Barnoldswick

The House

I'm standing before this house, queasy just looking at it, it's mangy and horrible. I've got to do what I've got to do. I'm inside looking around, walls with blood all over them and the lonely door at the end of the hallway. I'm opening the door right now …
Creak …

Caleb-James Parkinson (13)

West Craven High Technology College, Barnoldswick

The Girl Has Gone!

She was standing there in the yard, I saw her. She looked up. It was getting dark. I didn't want to stay, but I had to because I knew she was doing something. It got dark quickly. She just stood there. There was a bang and she was gone!

Robyn Hobson-Shaw (13)

West Craven High Technology College, Barnoldswick

Haunted School!

As I was walking in the ghoul-haunted school,
I was trembling to the bones of my toes. My
footsteps echoed down the dreaded hallways. My
body was chilly. It was so sombre that there only
stood one candle in the middle of the hallway.
Who had put it there?

Charlotte Crabtree (12)

West Craven High Technology College, Barnoldswick

The Haunted And Deadly School

As me, Chloe and Charlotte walked through the old, rotten door, we saw someone standing there that looked like a ghost. We ran over to the corner where it stood and it disappeared, but we saw a glimpse of it. It was gaunt, deadly and transparent. We followed it …

Sophie Halstead (13)

West Craven High Technology College, Barnoldswick

The Woods

I was walking the dog and it was very sombre.
The trees were rustling as I walked through the
woods. I had a feeling I was being followed. There
was a deadly screech. At this point I was lost. I
could hear footsteps. It was getting closer …
'Help, please help!'

Courtney Leah Wright (12)
West Craven High Technology College, Barnoldswick

My Last Journey

I was walking home from school alone, suddenly
feeling a cold breeze across my face. My heart
started beating out of my chest. I had that
awkward lump in my throat. Feeling anxious, I
turned to see that there was nothing but a slowly
fading shadow, then I saw a …

Maryam Raza (13)
West Craven High Technology College, Barnoldswick

Untitled

I heard a frightful scream up on a gigantic hill, so I dashed up there. While I was sprinting up the hill, I heard another frightful scream. I finally got to the top of the hill. There it was, an atrocious mansion, but what was inside?

Melissa Bradley (12)

West Craven High Technology College, Barnoldswick

Fate Of The Fallen

It has been two years since the great battle ended and the ruins of Ailar still stand as a testament to the fallen. But it's not over. Old enemies are astir. Nemesis, half man, half ghost, who ran away to live a life of solitude, must step forward yet again …

Gemma Wilkinson (13)

West Craven High Technology College, Barnoldswick

Indescribable

A savage scream ripped the night apart, a shriek so ear-piercing, so heart-rending, so full of despair that I would *never* forget! Stumbling, panicking and confused. Seeing the face grotesque, twisted into convulsions, neck streaming with gore, a waft of decay erupted from the mangled corpse. I gagged!

Tara Quinn (13)

West Craven High Technology College, Barnoldswick

Untitled

Whistling wind blowing the shrivelled trees at either side of the deformed house. The dark, overgrown grass, full of treacherous traps. The old windows were shattered with raggy curtains, full of cobwebs. The gate was rusty and old, it was taller than the house. The house was very eerie.

Loren Walling (12)

West Craven High Technology College, Barnoldswick

Untitled

As fast as I could, I ran, beads of sweat trickling
down my face. Dare I turn? What if it's true?
Why did I do it? I'm such an idiot! It can't be true,
ghosts aren't real! Maybe a peek. *Bang!*
Darkness …
All I hear is crying, barely, slowly fading …

Sarah Amer (12)

West Craven High Technology College, Barnoldswick

253

The Storm House

Crashing, howling, screeching, the storm was closing in on me. I knew I needed refuge in the old house, but either way I might not see daylight again. The house was a mystery to everyone, but nobody survived a night to tell the story. I twisted the handle …
I screamed!

Tyla Mackie (13)

West Craven High Technology College, Barnoldswick

Haunted House

Immediately, the rotten, musty, deadly smell hit me. That haunted house sitting in front of me, the six floors towering above me. A saggy door, with a decayed, rusty doorknob as big as my head, the windows blocked out with mould. I heard screeching - they had seen me standing there …

Shannon Boothman (13)

West Craven High Technology College, Barnoldswick

Horrors Of The Night

If there was any chance that this was just a sick, horrifying rumour, then I wouldn't be here. But I felt it. I could feel the ice-cold shimmering in the slight breeze, right here, in my own home town. But, despite all the danger, I stepped willingly into view …

Natasha Brammah (12)

West Craven High Technology College, Barnoldswick

Untitled

Tentatively tiptoeing, gnarled, blood-tainted
fingers slid down the savage, scratchy rope. My
footsteps echoed down the bridge. Loathsome
thoughts clawed my mind. Below lay a murderous
crime. Sea, black as ink, as murky as death,
enclosing the body. My victim! Peering round, its
spirit hovered, brandishing knives …
'Tig, you're it!'

Nikki Harper (12)
West Craven High Technology College, Barnoldswick

The Calling

He hated this place; the musty smell, bad memories sending shivers down his spine. Trembling fiercely, he sat. He knew what was coming. It stood there, dark, disturbing and eerie, yellow bloodstained fangs ready, casting a shadow over him. It wanted more than just blood, this time it wanted him …

Bethan Hawkins (12)

West Craven High Technology College, Barnoldswick

Dead!

I'm lying on the backstreet crippled, with red
stains covering my shirt. My hair, greasy and
rugged. My eyes, wide and desperate. My left leg
is replaced by pools of blood. Some poor kid will
find me in the middle of his morning paper round.
Ha! Someone's having nightmares tonight.

Sam Bugler (13)

West Craven High Technology College, Barnoldswick

The Package

Jumping over the barriers and ducking under the bridge, I hid from the shopkeeper that I had stolen it from. Just above me, I could hear him asking people if they had seen me. When I had caught my breath, I ran again. He shouted, but I was too quick.

Benjamin Clarke (12)

West Craven High Technology College, Barnoldswick

Shadow

Another ripple shuddered through my already
quivering body. Beads of sweat trickled down
my neck. I could feel the atmosphere. Someone,
somewhere, was watching me. But who? I
cautiously turned around and saw it, in the
shadows …
Big, cat-like hands reached out to grab me. I
turned and sprinted …

Emma Cutler (13)
West Craven High Technology College, Barnoldswick

261

The Mysterious Church

The time had come, I was approaching the dark,
mysterious church. What was I thinking? My dog
ran away a long time ago. I was rapidly closing
in on the church. I opened the door and a loud,
thunderous creak came from it. I looked directly
left. Someone was there ...

Luke Scothern (13)
West Craven High Technology College, Barnoldswick

The Church

The illuminated, stained glass window of the church was uncommon. Nobody used it anymore. I went to check it out! I went in. Nobody was there, but there was a noise from upstairs. I went up. Who was it? What was it? I went through the door. Would I survive?

Zack Allum-Spencer (12)
West Craven High Technology College, Barnoldswick

Untitled

The street illuminated. I was standing at the top
of the church tower. I knew at twelve it was
over! I heard footsteps coming from below. *Thud!
Thud! Thud! He's here,* I thought. *He's going to kill
me!* He peered round the door. I jumped to the
ground and ran …

Rebecca Bowers (12)

West Craven High Technology College, Barnoldswick

Untitled

I awoke, sat up and began to look around.
Where was I? One moment I was sitting in a giant
pool of blood, then it faded away and now this.
Everything was white. But how could it be? There
seemed to be no wall. I was somehow floating …

Amalia Kerkine-Keramida (13)

West Craven High Technology College, Barnoldswick

265

Graveyard, Gravestones

Slowly creeping in the shadowy darkness, I got nearer and nearer. Staring at the rotten gravestones and the gnarled trees, I panicked … I heard somebody's voice echoing, getting closer and closer. I screamed! I felt it touch me. What was it? Running rapidly, screeching, I realised that was my gravestone …

Chloe Utley (13)
West Craven High Technology College, Barnoldswick

The Haunted House Of Rustle Top Road

Monstrous and overpowering bats circled me. I crept towards the solid oak door. The garden was treacherous and musty. I endured it though! Tall, vandalised, eerie, decayed and frightful was the house. I placed my pale, trembling hand on the knob. I was in … but would I get back out?

Alex Holt (13)

West Craven High Technology College, Barnoldswick

Ferris Wheel

I looked down. The clouds danced around over
the Ferris wheel as the overpowering wind shook
the seats. A loud, shrill snapping sound occurred
as I reached the top. I panicked as I leaned
forward to see where it came from. The safety
bar jolted open and I tumbled out …

Ashleigh Brierley (13)
West Craven High Technology College, Barnoldswick

The Bush Monster

I was walking home from Sam's. The wind was blowing and the moon shone bright above me. The bushes seemed to communicate with each other. I moved in closer to see if I could hear. As I moved closer, the bushes rustled. I was frightened. I reached out and then …

Adam Rowley (13)
West Craven High Technology College, Barnoldswick

Apocalypse

As the storm got closer and closer, we had to enter the dark, dismal, safe house which stank of human urine, stale food and rotting corpses. Suddenly, a loud noise came from the roof of the safe house. The noise started to come down the stairs. Suddenly, it was there …

Tayler Handforth (12)

West Craven High Technology College, Barnoldswick

Footsteps

There were footsteps pounding down the corridor. I quickly turned my head. Slowly creeping, I peered down the hallway. There wasn't anyone there, yet I had the strangest sensation that I was not alone. I heard a creak of a floorboard from merely metres away. I felt an inhuman presence …

Oliver Beckwith (12)

West Craven High Technology College, Barnoldswick

271

The Empty Room

Bang! The sound echoed around the empty hall, breaking the still silence like a gunshot. No sound had been made in this room for years. The noise seemed to amplify as it bounced off the walls. The once brightly coloured walls were now dark and dingy. Something wasn't right …

Elspeth Adams (12)
West Craven High Technology College, Barnoldswick

Drop Dead Beautiful

In the shade, her beauty was utterly blinding. Everything about her was perfect - her face, her hair, her eyes, everything! But in a way she was too perfect. As she gracefully made her way over to me, I noticed something. Something wasn't right. As she stepped out into the sunlight …

Adele Duffin (12)
West Craven High Technology College, Barnoldswick

The Abandoned School

I climbed through the rubble towards the hazardous, abandoned school. As the eerie moon shone on the building, the true colours of the school showed. The walls were damp, deformed and rotten, but that wasn't the thing that caught my attention. A disgusting stench from the top, right-hand window …

Victoria Harris (12)

West Craven High Technology College, Barnoldswick

This Is Where The Tide Comes In

I looked back at my home. I looked over the cliff. It has been raining. I sat on the sodden grass looking down. I felt the hole in my chest opening up, spilling out my doubts and loneliness. I looked down at my broken body, 200ft below me ...

Emily Newsome (13)

West Craven High Technology College, Barnoldswick

275

Information

We hope you have enjoyed reading this book - and that you will continue to enjoy it in the coming years.

If you like reading and writing, drop us a line or give us a call and we'll send you a free information pack. Alternatively visit our website at **www.youngwriters.co.uk**

Write to:

Young Writers Information,
Remus House,
Coltsfoot Drive,
Peterborough,
PE2 9JX

Tel: (01733) 890066
Email: youngwriters@forwardpress.co.uk